You're <u>Not</u> Elected, Charlie Brown

You're <u>Not</u> Elected, Charlie Brown

by Charles M. Schulz

SCHOLASTIC BOOK SERVICES

New York Toronto London Auckland Syndey Tokyo

ISBN: 0-590-08820-3

12 11 10 9 8 7 6 5 4   0 1 2 3 4 5/8

Sally was mad. She stomped down the steps of her school and walked all the way home with a frown on her face.

She slammed the door of her house and shouted, "I'm never going to school again!"

"What's the matter?" asked Charlie Brown. "Is your teacher giving you trouble again? Don't you understand the math problems? Are the kids on the playground giving you trouble?"

"No," said Sally. "There is nothing wrong with my teacher, and I got 100 on a math test yesterday and I get along fine with the rest of the kids."

"Well, then, what's the trouble?" asked Charlie Brown.

"I can't get my stupid locker open!" said Sally.

Next day, when they got to school, Charlie Brown said, "Which one's your locker? I'll help you get it open."

Sally dragged Charlie Brown right past the lockers and said, "Forget that for now. I need your help in my first class."

She sat down at her desk, with her brother standing rather awkwardly in the aisle, and then she raised her

hand to attract the teacher's attention. "Miss Othmar," she said, "I volunteer to be first."

Before Charlie Brown knew what was happening, he found himself up in front of the whole class while Sally began to use him as the subject for Show & Tell.

"This morning, fellow classmates," she said, "I have a treat for you. I am showing you my big brother. And I should tell you that he's my big brother only because he was lucky enough to be born first." Then she leaned over to Charlie Brown and whispered, "Stand up straight—I'm trying to get an 'A' in Show & Tell. Don't goof it for me!"

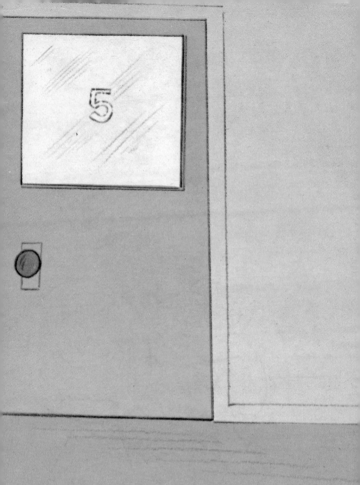

When the ordeal was over, Charlie Brown walked down one of the halls in the school, and said to himself,

"That has to be the most embarrass-
ing thing that's ever happened to me
in my whole life."

A group of children was standing in the hall, looking at a huge sign announcing the coming election of a student body president. When Linus saw Charlie Brown, he said, "This would be a good job for you. You'd make a great student body president."

Just then, Lucy came walking up.

"No," Lucy said, "I have already
taken a poll, and my poll shows that
Charlie Brown could never be
elected. No one would ever say,

'You're elected, Charlie Brown,' because there is no way you could ever be elected. So we'll have to find another candidate."

Sally had just joined the group and she asked, "How about Linus? I'll bet he'd do something about those stupid lockers."

"Well, I don't know," said Lucy, "but I'll take another poll and find out."

Lucy's polls were sometimes kind of violent. She grabbed one boy by the shirt and said, "If my brother Linus were running for student body president, would you vote for him?"

"How could I help it?" he answered.

The next little boy said, "Sure I'd vote for Linus, I remember one time he gave me half of his peanut-butter sandwich. I'd vote for anybody who gave me lunch."

The next person to be interviewed was a rather ordinary looking little boy who was sitting by himself on a small bench. Lucy said to him, "If you

knew that Linus Van Pelt were running for president, would you vote for
him?"

"No," said the boy.

"If you knew that he was going to solve all the problems of the world, would you vote for him?"

"No," said the boy.

"But why not!" shouted Lucy.

"Because I'm the one who is running against him!"

"I think we're in," said Lucy as she reported back to her candidate. "According to my poll, there is no way we can lose."

And so the big campaign began. It was Charlie Brown's job to introduce the two candidates to the rest of the students during an assembly period.

When Linus's rival was introduced he said, "My name is Russell Anderson, and if I'm elected I will do the best I can. Thank you."

"That's the worst speech I've ever heard," said Lucy, "Now I know we're going to win."

Charlie hired Snoopy to do some posters.

Snoopy went to Woodstock for help.

They did a great job.

Lucy arranged to have Linus be on a talk show.

But she did most of the talking herself.

"Will you change things around here?" he was asked.

"I'm not sure . . ." began Linus.

"He's not sure what he'll do first," interrupted Lucy, "but as president, Linus plans to tell the principal that we don't want any more tests. And no report cards. And no homework. Right Linus?"

"Right," Linus replied weakly.

The day before the election, Linus and Russell Anderson went before the entire student body to give their final speech. They cheered Linus when he stepped forward.

"I have appreciated your support during my campaign," he began. "Therefore I have a little surprise for you. Rather than bore you with more campaign talk, I have decided that today I would say a few words about the Great Pumpkin."

Suddenly the auditorium erupted with laughter, and Linus realized he had said the wrong thing.

"Oh, you blockhead!" cried Lucy. "There was no way we could lose until now! We had it won for sure, but now we'll be lucky if we get half the votes!"

And she was right. The election was very close. After each of the students had dropped his secret ballot into the box, Charlie Brown read the results off to Schroeder and Violet, who were keeping the count. It was close all the way.

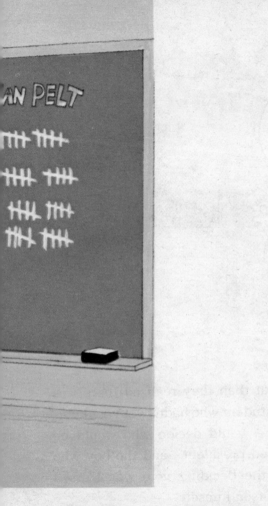

Finally, the balloting stood 83 votes for Russell Anderson and 83 votes for Linus Van Pelt.

But then they realized there was one student who hadn't yet voted. His choice would decide who would be elected president—and the boy who had the deciding vote was Russell Anderson himself.

"We're doomed,' cried Lucy.

Russell dropped his ballot in the box.

Charlie Brown announced the result. "One more vote for Linus."

"I think he would make a better president than I would," explained Russell.

Everyone was happy, but Sally was ecstatic. She grabbed Linus by the hand and rushed him off to the principal's office. "Now you can do all of the things you said you were going to do, Linus. Now you have the authority. We voted you in."

But when he came out of the office, Linus explained to Sally that he probably wouldn't be able to do as much as he had thought.

"The principal still runs the school," said Linus.

"You sold out!" Sally shrieked. "We elected you, and you sold out! The next time we have an election, I think everyone should vote for himself. Or we might just as well vote for Charlie Brown! Yes, next year we may even say, 'You're elected, Charlie Brown!'"